Twelve Acres

Written and Illustrated
by Jason Down

All characters in this publication are fictitious and any resemblance to real persons, living, or dead, is purely coincidental

A catalogue record for this book is available from the British Library

ISBN 978-0-9929144-5-5

www.Bonkerbooks.com

When Smithy decides to teach his son the true meaning of fishing, and Jenny the philosophical fish takes the young carp, called Georgie under her fin, two worlds collide.

Twelve Acres

A small carp is released into a strange new world. Cautiously, he swims through the weeds into a clearing, where the silence is shattered.

"Incoming, we got incoming!" cries the on duty roach.

Fish of all sizes scatter in different directions, dodging what seems like a million missiles hitting the water. Panic stricken, the carp dives back into the closest weed bed for cover. Slowly, calm returns to the clearing, and the small fish peers out of the weed. The place is now buzzing with fish feeding on large balls of food. Hungry, and with a sense of relief, the carp goes to join them.

"Hold on little fellow, if you want to avoid capture, let the bream and roach feed first."

"Capture, what's capture?" The little carp looked up at a bigger built carp.

"Say, you must be new around here, you got a name kid?"

"My name's G, short for Georgie."

"Pleased to meet you G, I'm Jenny. Now watch carefully."

G turned his attention back to the feeding frenzy. In disbelief, G saw one of the larger bream being pulled towards the surface. "What's happening?"

"They've been hooked," Jenny responded, "None of us know Why but the gods do like to play games with us.

"What are gods?" G made Jenny laugh.

"You really are naive," Jenny frowned, "come on, let me show you around. I'd hate to see anything..."

"Look there's another carp feeding," G, interrupted, "does that mean it's safe to feed?" G, moved closer to the food.

"Slow down, G," Jenny smiled, "He's always getting caught, and desperate to reach sixty pounds in order not to spend any more time on the bank."

"What's time on the bank?'" G, called back.

"Oh my, Lewy," Jenny called to one of the feeding fish, "can you come over here please."

"Hi Jenny," Lewy swam over to her, "are you not eating…?

You'll never gain weight fasting. You see that guy over there?"

Jenny looked in the direction of the large roach stuffing himself.

"Sure…"

"He comes to the weight gain group every week, but I doubt, he'll ever make the grade."

"Look," Jenny cried, "there he goes…"

Much, to G's shock they all watched the large roach struggle against the upward pull.

"How did you know that was going to happen?" Lewy remarked.

"Let's just call it a hunch." Jenny paused, "I want you to meet G, the new kid. What do you reckon he weighs?"

"I'd say no more than three pounds." Lewy stared hard at G. "Listen kid, if you're going to survive the summer, you'll have to bulk up a bit."

"What do you mean survive?" G's comment amused Lewy.

"Don't listen to him," Jenny soothed, "he's just kidding. C'mon, I'll show you around."

"I'm not joking," but, before Lewy could continue, Jenny begun shepherding G, away.

"Why did he say survive?" G, asked.

"The pond does have its fair share of hazards, but if you learn from me, and gain some weight, you'll find there's nothing to fear."

"What about these gods?" G, asked.

"Even the gods, can be fooled." Jenny looked up at a large shadow that appeared on the surface.

...

Smithy, and his son Dash, carried their fishing kit across the meadow. It would be his son's first fishing trip. Approaching Twelve Acre Lake, Smithy paused to assess the view. Dug out in the eighteenth century, the whole area had matured into a natural beauty spot. The far side of the lake lived in the shadow of large oaks, ashes and willows, before sweeping around to the widest part of the water. The bank was broken only now and then by old trees, that served as shade for the fishermen in the height of the summer. The narrow end was a series of deep snag filled inlets, where countless trees had given way to the prevailing wind, perfect for the wildlife. It was for this reason, that Twelve Acre was Smithy's favourite fishing water.

"Hey, dad," Dash said, spying a familiar face not so far away, "can we say hi to uncle, Paul?"

"Calm down Dash," Smithy could sense his son's excitement.

"Remember what I told you about staying quiet and relaxed, it's what makes a good fisherman."

"Uncle Paul!" Dash called out running towards him.

"Hey Dash, you finally made it then did you?"

Uncle Paul had a booming voice along with a customary laugh that accompanied each sentence. "So, your dad is finally going to teach you how to roach fish?"

Dash smiled at his uncle, "we aren't after roach uncle, Paul. I'm going to catch the legendary, sixty pounder!"

Uncle Paul roared with laughter. "Your dad, what a guy, on his old school rods you're limited."

"They've never let me down," Smithy interrupted having just caught them up, "besides, there's more to fishing than fancy rods."

Uncle Paul paused, then in thought rubbed his chin. "Let me show you something kid."

Dash followed his uncle towards a platform where his rods were set up.

"Wow, I've never seen..."

"A set up like it..." Uncle Paul interrupted, "let me explain what we got." Paul turned and pointed, "These are the XP, 3000, long range, carp ascenders. Three and a half pound test curve rods, with matching, XP, 360, any range, optimal, super light bait runners. In other words, we are big game hunting."

"Dad, did you hear that." Dash turned to his dad and back again. "Uncle Paul your set up is the coolest, but what's all that kit in the boat for?"

Uncle Paul laughed again, “ground bait. I’ve put 15k out this morning. Once I get past the bream and roach, we’ll see some big carp.”

“Come on Dash, you can speak to your uncle later.” Smithy nodded good luck to Paul, before moving on.

“See you later kid.” Paul shouted after them.

“Dad you said we had to be quiet around the water, but uncle Paul shouts, laughs and…”

“Shhhhhhhhhh.” His father hushed him while staring across the lake.

“What is it dad?” Smithy stared at a lean man on the other side of the bank.

“Is that him dad?”

“Yes, that’s Dave Buzz, the one I’ve told you about?”

Dash felt a shiver run down his back. Dave Buzz was well known to everyone who fished Twelve Acre. His dad saw him as a trophy hunter, with little or no respect, for the environment, fish, and least of all, other fishermen.

Dave, held the lake record, but had nearly killed the catch due to the length of time he'd kept the fish out the water. But, his main obsession was the sixty pound legend, and Dave, was prepared to use any tactic to get it. Rumours of foul play were writhe. Lines had been cut during the night fishing. And soap, to flush fish from the overhanging trees, had all been spotted. But most of all, Dave was renowned for casting into other people`s swims, and on account of his foul temper, very few confronted him.

"Dash, over here, this will do us."

The swim, and view, was everything his father had ever described, right down to the large heron that squawked when they moved it on. Slowly, Smithy begun to set up the rods, for what he hoped, would be a glorious morning.

"Everything washes up at the bar kid." G did his best to keep up while listening to Jenny, "so food isn't hard to find," she continued, "but, watch yourself, the early morning gets pretty busy."

Gliding through some weeds towards a clearing, a large bank of gravel stretched as far as G's eyes could see. Fish, of all sizes mingled, but it was the clawed creatures that caught his eye.

"Those guys you're staring at," Jenny explained, "are the crays. They collect food and check it for hooks. For me, the price is too high. Come on," Jenny turned, "this way G."

"What are hooks Jenny?" G asked whilst dodging some large bream in a hurry.

"Hooks are all part of this game the gods like to play. If you're going to avoid being pulled to the surface, you will have to learn the art of checking your food first."

"Have you ever been hooked Jenny?"

"Only once," Jenny sighed, "luckily, I was able to break the pull, but it took me two weeks to shed the hook because of where it was. That's one of the reasons I keep fit and don't grow a belly like Lewy. You see there are two trains of thought, one, is to use sheer size to break the hold, but the trouble with using weight, is that you tire too quickly. The other, is staying trim, and at a good size like me, so you can fight harder."

Jenny continued to explain her theory as they moved along the bar towards two large bream.

"Hey guys," she asked eyeing the red bait balls before them. "Do you know if this food came in recently?"

The larger fish looked rather annoyed at being disturbed.

"Do we really look like waiters?" His reply was sharp as he glided away.

"Gosh, some fish just have no manners!" Jenny turned her attention back towards the pile of small food balls. Gently, she nosed it about before sucking up the food. Then, much to G's shock, she spat it back out.

"What's the matter," G, enquired in surprise, "is the food no good?"

"Yes, but I'm Just checking for hooks. It's safe," said Jenny, "so tuck in if you like."

Not having eaten that morning, G was delighted.

"You see, down here, G, you'll have to show some self-control by always checking the food."

In between stuffing his face, G, wondered how fish got hooked if they always checked their food. This, he put to Jenny.

"That's a good question. Most fish do check their food, but fish in general, have one big flaw, especially carp."

...

“What is it?”

“Well, it’s commonly known as frenzy.”

“Frenzy…?”

“Yes, frenzy. It’s a kind of condition where for some reason, the fish lose all sense of reality, gorging blindly and stuffing their stomachs silly, until one of them gets hooked. No one really knows why. But, most fish fall to this condition at breakfast and tea time. Only old Birdie offers any real explanation, he’s the lakes oldest resident.”

“What is this food?” G, smiled in delight, “I’ve, never eaten

anything this tasty before, no wonder fish get carried away."

"These are a gift from the god's to entice us."

Just then, headed by the largest carp, G, had ever seen, a huge shoal of fish came up from the bar.

"It's ok G, that's the Caesium carp shoal headed by Tyson. He's the biggest carp in the pond, also the most arrogant. Oh, and those," Jenny turned towards some of the cray fish, "are really good food testers."

Slowly, the shoal backed up to Jenny and retested the food.

"Hey, you guys," the largest of the cray fish shouted, "I guarantee you the foods is all good."

Tyson turned and stared hard at the cray. "Do you think I trust you, you low life! Just gather the food and keep your mouth shut."

"Someday Tyson," the cray fish mused, "your arrogance, will be your undoing."

G, was surprised the cray fish didn't back down.

Tyson moved menacingly forward until his nose met the cray. "But not today…!"

Jenny gestured, that they move on, but G, couldn't help but look back. Holding his gaze for a few seconds, Tyson stared hard at G.

G turned to catch Jenny. "Why does the carp check his food like that?"

"Tyson is one of the elders and pretty much runs the gravel

bars. Not much gets past him, that's for sure. Deep down, he's not a bad guy, but we all stay out of his way. You'd do well to do the same."

At the far end of the bar another feeding frenzy appeared to be in progress. Amongst the fish, was big, Lewy.

"I might have known," Jenny sighed.

"Hey," Lewy cried out, "its Jenny and the new kid, you want some corn?"

Much to the delight of the roach, even more corn rained down and was scattered upon the floor.

"C'mon," Lewy insisted, "the gods are giving it away today look around."

While G tucked in with big Lewy, Jenny patiently observed the shadow above them.

...

Uncle Paul poured buckets of bait from his boat, out over the gravel bar, pausing from time to time to laugh. From the bank, watching him carefully was Dash.

"Hey dad, can we throw some bait out?"

"Over baiting a swim like that son, isn't always a good thing. In fact, if the food isn't eaten, it can become poisonous to the fish."

Seeing his son's deflated face, Smithy, brushed the hover flies from the air and pulled a catapult from his pocket.

"If you want Dash, you can fire some boilies out with this." Instantly, Dash's face once again lit up.

"Here, aim them at the lilies."

Dash had never used a catapult before and his first effort flew wide of the lilies, nearly knocking a wood pigeon from its perch. His second effort was weak, falling well short of his target. Finally, he pulled the elastic back as far as he could.

"This time," Dash told himself, "this time."

Much to his horror, the bait flew past the lilies and towards Dave Buzz. Striking his leg, the lean Dave Buzz stood up and looked at Dash in disgust.

"Dad, I think I may have over shot that one." Smithy stared back, until muttering to himself, Dave sat down.

"Sorry Dad." Dash lowered his head.

"It's not your fault son, here, let me show you." Smithy spent the next ten minutes teaching Dash, how to fire baits accurately. A few minutes later, a light shower sprinkled the water, forcing Smithy, to put up his brolly. Rain pattered on the umbrella, coupled with sunshine, it produced a faint rainbow. But, as the welcome wonder petered out the hover flies returned.

"Dad," shouted Dash, "uncle, Paul's caught something."

Smithy smiled knowingly at the bend in the rod.

"I don't think it's a fish son."

Dash watched his uncle pull a large branch from the water followed by the usual boom of laughter. Dash readdressed his own float. Little and often, his father had told him when throwing in baits. So, why hadn't he had a bite?

...

"So, G," Lewy asked still scoffing large mouthfuls of food. "What do you make of your new home?"

"It's different," G, felt bashful, "there were no gods in my last home, and when it came to feeding, the food was always found floating on top."

"So," Lewy enquired, "how did you end up here?"

"One minute I was swimming with the fish, the next being pulled up by a large net. From there, we were put into small containers." G, paused, "then, before I knew it, I was released in here and met Jenny."

"Jenny is a great girl." Both fish looked over to where she was feeding, "you're lucky she's taken you under her fin."

A crowd of carp descended and joined Jenny. From the shoal, two pretty mirror carp appeared. Not much bigger than G, one of them caught his eye and made him blush.

Noticing G's reaction, Jenny smiled. "C'mon G, it's time to show you around, before the gods start to cast their traps."

"Where are we heading?"

"I thought we could explore the lilies, and see what foods available on top."

"Cool," G looked at Lewy, "see you later."

Jenny, led G, into the open water and picked up a shallow trench. As they travelled along the road, G, noticed, that not only, was the water getting deeper, but colder too. Her senses on full alert, Jenny swam rather vigorously.

"Is everything ok?" G, asked.

"This is the start of Cat Alley," she finally whispered, "most of the catfish are fine, but there's Devlan, a hundred pound monster who eats just about anything, including small carp."

"Small carp…?" G, gulped, moving much closer to Jenny.

"Don't worry, we only need to follow it a short way," Jenny Comforted, G, "this route, then, leads to the snags."

Swimming clear of Cat Alley, the two fish gently drifted up to the surface, until under the shelter of a large lily pad area.

"G, push your head through the pads like this."

Jenny nuzzled the surface before poking her head back down. "There's all manner of natural food to be found G."

Jenny moved peacefully about the pads searching for flies and insects. Quickly, G copied. Noticing two more carp, he watched them feed freely around the fringe of the lilies.

"Jenny, what about the edges…?"

"Learn the ropes first G, there are ways to feed on top which I will show you. For now, just enjoy the security from the pads."

…

Back on the bank, binoculars in his hand, Smithy observed the movement around the lilies. He also sensed the boredom, Dash was feeling. So, going to his fishing bag, he put together his surface feeding rod.

"Dash," Smithy looked at him, "I think it's time for a change in tactics. What, say we go stalking around the lilies?"

Eager, Dash lit up. "We'll have to be quiet though Dash, bring the net and bait bag, let's go catch a carp."

The midday sunshine on them, they slowly moved around the lake.

"Dad," Dash was excited, "I can see some carp over there."

"Shhhhhhhhhh, Dash. Remember what I said about staying Quiet…?" Smithy knelt and pointed at the water, "remember earlier Dash, when I showed you to use the catapult?" Dash nodded. "Well, here's your chance to fire some bread out to the lilies."

As Dash landed some bread amongst the lilies, the delight displayed on his face made Smithy happy.

Both nestling down amongst the undergrowth, they didn't have to wait long for the first carp to start feeding.

"Dad they're taking it!" Dash whispered.

"Pass me the rod son." With real perfection, Smithy molded a piece of bread to his hook, allowing just enough crust so it would still float. Then, with an expert cast, landed the bread six inches shy of the pads.

"Wow," impressed with his dads casting, Dash settled down and watched for any movements.

…

G was bored, and turned his attention back to the two large carp milling near the edge. Even more so, when a fat chunk of food landed there. Transfixed, G, casually cruised towards it, but, Jenny stopped nosing for flies, and blocked his path.

"G, what are you doing?"

"About to eat," he answered sarcastically, "those carp over there," he looked ahead, "have been feeding for ages with no problems."

"I'm leaving," Jenny turned away, "either come with me," she said looking back at him, "or stay here on your own."

G, watched her swim away, and wondered why she'd shown so much caution over one piece of bread.

"I'll eat this then catch her up." G, said to himself. Turning, he saw one of the large carp poised below the food.

"Hey you guys, I was about to eat that."

The larger of the two fish looked at G. "Son, I'll be amazed if you can even fit in your mouth, so why don't you run along and play with the roach."

The carp grinned and sucked in the food. But his expression quickly changed, and the water erupted.

"Swim for it, we got a taker." The other carp cried out.

...

On the bank, Smithy struck hard. The line tore from the real, and the bend in his rod told him it was a good fish.

"Dad you got one!" Excited, Dash, watched his dad play the fish.

"Stay calm Dash, put that net together and wait there. This one's going to take a while." Over the next ten minutes, Smithy played the fish. "Let it run when it needs to," he shouted to Dash, "never try and bully a fish," you hear me son?" Smithy then placed the net under the tired carp, "it's a good fish Dash." Smithy lifted it up the bank and onto the unhooking mat.

"Wow, it's a whopper Dad!" Smithy gently eased the hook out, a moment later, Dash felt overshadowed.

"Uncle Paul," he said glancing round, "dads caught a monster!"

"He sure has..." Uncle, Paul, watched Smithy lift the fish onto his scales.

"Sixteen ounces…!" Smithy squealed, "I'd say we got a thirty two pound mirror carp."

Uncle Paul, took a photo of them both, Smithy, then, nursed the fish back into the water.

"Right you two," uncle, Paul beamed, "let's have a bite to eat round my bivvy."

There, while Dash listened to uncle, Paul recounting fishing stories, Smithy, observed Dave Buzz. Perched on a long willow branch, Dave was leant over the water. He was patiently watching two large carp bask in the afternoon sun, when, out of the depths, rose an enormous fish. An icy stillness set in Dave's body. The sheer size of the carp confirmed that it had to be the legend. Gently, Dave lowered some bait onto the water leaving no trace of his line. As the fish drifted closer, Dave expressed delight. But, as another large carp approached, his grin disappeared. "No, no," he muttered to himself. Forced to strike hard, the line was torn from Dave's reel and the fish swallowed his bait. In an attempt to slow the large carp down, Dave tightened the clutch on his reel. Stretched to his limit, the branch began to bend. Quickly, Smithy, Dash, and uncle, Paul, stood up with their mouths open. The limb continued to bow, before giving way with an almighty crack. Crashing into the water, Dave and his rod disappeared. Resurfacing, his rod was gone along with the fish. Fury on his face, Dave Buzz began to thrash the water. Young Dash, looked utterly shocked at what he'd witnessed, even more so when his uncle burst into fits of laughter. "Good old Dave, there's nothing that man won't do for the record!"

In his panic, G, found himself in unfamiliar territory, and cursed himself for not listening to Jenny.

"Pssst, hey kid, you look kind of lost."

Turning one way then the other, G, couldn't work out where the voice had come from.

"Over here kid..." Much to G's surprise, a long nosed fish appeared from the weed, "I'm Jasper, and you look like you could use some help?"

As the fish emerged fully from the weeds, G's, gut feeling was to swim, but he didn't.

"I guess I could do with a little direction," G, mumbled, "I'm heading for the gravel bar, but have lost my way."

"The gravel bar…?" The long fish grinned exposing some sharp white teeth, "well, it just so happens, I know a short cut."

Beckoning G, to follow, the long fish turned. His options limit, G obliged. The long fish led him into the weeds until, they came to what looked like a gate way. Passing through, G saw that it was actually the jaw bone of a very large fish.

A clearing ahead revealed more lanky fish. Growing closer, G, begun to regret his decision, and was soon surrounded by a small crowd.

"Hey," a fish not much bigger than G, called out, "who's your new friend?"

"This is…?" the long fish turned to face G, "I didn't catch your name son?"

"I'm G," he said uneasily, "your friend is showing me the way to the gravel bar."

"Sure he is," the conversation was snapped up by a larger fish, "the gravel bar hmm," the fish boomed in amusement, "well, first you've got to pay the toll, or take the test."

"Pay, what's pay?" G, felt disturbed by the laughter all around him.

"Looks like we got a new contender for our little challenge lads." The large fish gloated.

"What is this test, and what if I fail?"

G's innocence, invited more laughter. Then, teeth revealed the big fish looked to the far side of the clearing. There, G saw a large pile of bones.

"You become dinner; now lock him up with the rest of to-night's supper."

G, looked around, but all the exits had been cut off by vicious looking fish.

"Come on, follow me," a fat spiny fish said, "There's a big test ahead." The fish rallied G, towards a narrow cage made from bones and weeds. His eyes were small and dark and stared straight ahead. "Go on, in you go."

Begrudgingly, G, entered. He heard the gate slam, then…

"You'll make a fine supper you will."

Chuckling, the fish swam back to the clearing.

In a state of shock, G sunk to the floor.

"How could I have been so stupid?" His heart skipping a beat, he then heard a voice.

"You're a carp," looking into the gloom a small silvery fish with two scars appeared, "how did you end up here?"

"Well, I'm new to the water," G, gazed beyond the bars at the fish, who had tricked him, "and I thought that fish was trying to help me."

"Who, Jasper, the pike?" the features of the silver fish became frightful, "you've got to be kidding me kid…!"

"Pike… Is that what they are?" said G, with a nauseated expression. "Are they really that devious?"

"They are more than that," the fish said unsmiling, "over thirty others were put in here with me," he peered into the depths of the empty cage, "I'm the last one."

"Did they have to do the test?" G cried loudly, "Perhaps," he whispered hopefully, "some of them passed and went free."

"There is no test," the fish felt terrible at delivering this news. "Just supper, with the fastest predators you'll ever meet."

The silver roach looked out of the bars and at the others.

"Oh, and a few obese fish, so say your prayers kid."

A strange humming suddenly drew their attention. "You hear that kid?" The silver fish perked up.

"What is it…?" G quickly quizzed. Peering into the gloom, he saw a silhouette materialize, "that, looks like Lewy."

"It is Lewy," the silver roach gulped, "but what's he doing here?"

Alert, the pike watched as the fish came crashing into the clearing. G, was about to call out, when he saw a silver spear chasing after Lewy. Shooting over his head, the spear crashed through the holding facility, where it destroyed the cage and freed the fish.

"Swim for it kid." But within minutes the big pike and three other fish were on their tails.

"They're gaining on us!" G, called after the roach.

In order to give G, a chance, the roach changed direction. "Keep going kid," he shouted back, "I'll see you on the other side."

Two of the pursuer's swiveled after the roach, but not the big pike. Within snapping distance, G, breathed his last. Then a strange thing happened. The object, still chasing Lewy lodged on a large snag. Then, as if by magic was catapulted backwards knocking the pike sideways like a skittle. Breathless, G finally felt it safe to stop and turn around.

"Are you ok Lewy?" G asked the dazed looking fish.

"A little bit bruised, but compared to him," Lewy, gazed at the stunned, but, still thunderous looking fish, "I think I'm going to live." He looked quizzically at G, "What the hell are you doing in this neighborhood? Do you want to be somebody's supper? Come, on, let's get out of here, before he comes round."

"Lewy," G, asked him, "what, was that thing chasing you?"

"Ha. It wasn't chasing me. I was pulling it. I got myself hooked. Only this time, I pulled the rod clean out of his hands, and judging by the sound, I'd say the fishermen came with it." Lewy paused in mid swim, "so, how did you end up in the predator's den, and where's Jenny?"

G, looked very sheepish, continuing to swim he explained the day's events.

"I know one thing," Lewy said, "Jenny may be stubborn, but you couldn't find yourself a more caring guide. Come on, let's find her."

...

As time turned into evening, Smithy savored a good day. Still as a mill pond, the lake glistened, until, slowly, the sun sunk behind the trees. But the spell was broken by the sound of Paul's laughing.

"Hey Dash," Paul was naturally loud, "did, you manage to catch anything in the end?"

"I, caught a big tench didn't I dad?" Smithy nodded approvingly and listened as Dash retold his story. "So," Dash finally asked, "what did you catch uncle, Paul?"

Paul paused, rubbed his chin, and glanced at Smithy. "Sure are a lot of roach in here."

"And what about Dave Buzz?" Smithy smirked making them all boom with laughter.

...

Lewy, looked for Jenny, and told her what had happened.

He then called G, over to face her.

"I think, this young man's got something to say."

"I'm sorry Jenny." But before he could say another word, she raised her fin.

"No, G, it's me who should be sorry. Leaving you like that wasn't fair."

"Lewy saved my life," G, looked sheepishly at the floor before looking up at Jenny, "does that mean I get another chance?" Jenny smiled warmly at G, then the gravel bar that was alive with feeding fish.

"I knew you guys would make up," Lewy said earnestly, "let's celebrate carp style." Lewy, moved towards a mound of coloured food, "tuck in guys!"

Jenny and G, laughed as he sucked it up.

...

Smithy, stopped to admire the water, the sun, yet to rise, dawn was the perfect moment.

"Come on dad," Dash interrupted full of excitement, "let's dump our gear and go to the tackle shop."

"Dash, can you hear that?" Smithy hushed his son.

"Hear what?" Dash looked bewildered.

"The silence before the sun comes up." There was an inspiring tone to Smithy's voice. "And, were the only people on the lake."

"Ah, but we are not alone dad, in fact, someone's in our swim Look?"

Smithy looked to his left. Indeed, someone had beaten them to their pre-baited swim. That someone was Dave Buzz. Dave was renowned for watching where people had baited the night before. He would then arrive early to steal the swim, then, to top it all, even had the cheek to smile in their direction. A look of disbelief appeared on Smithy's face.

"Come on Dash, there's plenty of good fishing on the main gravel bar."

"But dad…"

It was too late his dad was already moving on. Smithy knew the lake well, and felt confident he could find somewhere else for Dash to fish. On the far bank, where Paul had anchored their boat, Smithy settled back down. From there, he showed Dash how to set up his rod, while at the same time overseeing his sons first hook knot. A king fisher arrived, cheeky and defiant, it approached Dash's bait box. As it straddled nearer, Dash's heart missed a beat, he blinked, and the bird flew away.

"Hey, Dash," Smithy, said desperately trying to lift his sons disappointment, "how about we row some bait out?"

"Definitely, cool!" Dash was excited, having watched his uncle the previous day he had no doubt, that the boat would be fun. Slowly, Dash and Smithy, stepped into the boat and sat either end of it.

"As I row," Smithy handed Dash a bucket of bait, "throw some handfuls of this from the back of the boat." Smithy then took up the oars. "We should, have enough to go up and down a few times if you don't go mad."

"Ok dad!" Pleased with the task, Dash begun baiting.

…

Below the surface, G woke late. Startled somewhat by the emptiness of the bar, he looked around.

To his left, observing a large shadow from above was Jenny.

"What is it?" G, asked in a slightly scared tone.

"The gods," Lewy answered joining them, "they freak most fish out, but as I, and Jenny have learnt, if you wait a while, you can feed in peace, and if lucky, tag some traps."

"But, where are all the other fish? G wanted more assurance.

"So far," said Jenny, "only Lewy, and I, have worked this out. Once that shadow leaves, this place will be buzzing again."

"Here we go G," Lewy announced, "follow the food and eat all you can..."

Sure enough food begun to filter from above, and the three fish started to feed on sweet scented offerings. Up and down they followed the trail, until the shadow stopped. Lewy then signaled for the other fish to be still.

"Now what…?" G, whispered.

"Once the food stops," Lewy insisted, "it usually means they will set traps."

They watched a single bait follow a silver stone down to the bottom. Jenny highlighted the trap with weed for the other fish to spot. Suddenly, the sound of a second trap broke the water and made G, jump.

"They're getting craftier," said Lewy, "that's for sure."

"How do you mean?" G was inquisitive.

"They've set the second trap where we can't see it," Jenny said in a sharp tone, "so we can't tag it."

Outsmarted on this occasion, Jenny was obviously annoyed.

"Hey," Lewy suggested, "let's take G, to the shallows, he'll enjoy sun bathing in the warmer water."

"Ok," Jenny agreed, "but no showing off, I mean it. Hang on." Clocking a couple of cray fish moving along the bar, she called out. "That bait's tagged," she warned them.

But, ignoring her, the two fish continued towards it. Chuckling, they removed the weed. Then, for their amusement, they waited for a victim to become hooked.

"There's gratitude," Jenny said as they swam away.

...

As Smithy moored the boat, Dash, became curious.

"Hey dad, did you see all the bubbles that followed the boat? Do you think they were carp following us, eating our baits as I threw them in?"

"Son, carp are intelligent, but that's going too far."

The thought that carp could outwit him, in this manner, amused Smithy.

"Then how do you explain the bubbles?" Dash persisted.

Unable to offer an explanation, Smithy busied himself with his kit instead. Dash was holding the rod, when he saw a solemn face sailing towards them.

"Hey dad, I thought Dave Buzz was fishing the far side?"

Tying a new rig together Smithy, saw Dave place a marker some fifteen yards short of his own baits. Typical Dave, he thought, the man has no patience, following every splash or bubble that surfaced. A few years back Dave had rowed out in a quest to land the legend. Quite unexpectedly, a large cat fish took his bait on the drop. The powerful fish then towed him along the water straight into the snags.

Dave would not let go of his rod, and the boat, was fractured causing it to sink into the deepest part of the lake, where it still was. The sound of Dash's bite alarm quickly drew them both back into focus.

"Strike it Dash," Smithy yelled. The boy struck hard.

"I'm in dad, I'm in," Dash repeated.

"Stay calm, let the fish run if it needs too, don't, force it..."

But the line went slack, leaving Dash no choice but to reel in.

"I think, I lost it." Drawing his own conclusions, Smithy observed the bend in his son´s rod.

"You haven't lost it Dash." He smiled, "I think you've hooked a bream."

"A bream…!" Dash continued to reel excitedly. Then, shaped like a dustbin lid, Smithy lifted the fish from the water and into their net.

"Wow, its huge Dad, and it didn't fight at all?"

"That's bream for you, son," he smiled, "it looks like a good one."

…

Below the surface, the three carp arrived in the warmer water. The temptation too much, Lewy swam upwards, shrieked and broke the surface. A minute later, he came crashing back down.

"Cool," G was amazed, "that looks great fun. Can I try?"

"See what you've started," Jenny stared at Lewy, "you know it attracts unwanted attention."

"Come on Jenny, live a little let the kid at least have a try."

G, thrust upwards, barely breaking the surface, he created a silly spat.

"Not that easy, hey kid." Lewy roared with laughter.

While Lewy, tried to show G, how to make a big splash, Jenny relaxed in the warm waters.

Their antics however, quickly drew the attention of Dave buzz.

"Incoming, we got incoming." Lewy shouted excitedly.

The food hit the surface, jolting Jenny from her relaxation. G, watched the sack of food drift to the bottom, then, as if by magic, the thin sack, dissolved, and revealed a pile of food.

"Wow, can we eat this?" G made Lewy laugh.

"Not so fast, if you want the food little guy you first have to trigger the trap." Lewy looked at Jenny, "after you."

"What's the trap?" G was becoming impatient.

"Watch carefully." Jenny nosed the food about, picking up some of the round baits then dropping them. She finally held one in her mouth, then, with one swift motion, fired the bait away. G was amazed to see the trap move like lightning back towards the surface.

"That was brilliant," G, gasped, "but, how did you know?"

"The way it works goes like this," Jenny spoke with her mouth Full. "Whenever a parcel enters the water, it will contain a trap. Through practice, we have learned to identify, then, trigger it. The food is then yours." Her voice deepened, "Practice, G, it takes practice."

Looking up, Jenny saw she had been talking to herself. "Lewy," she asked him, "where's G?"

A blank look on his face, Lewy fumbled for an answer.

"Oh no..." Jenny, suddenly spied G.

Sifting through a second pile of food, he was attempting to find the trap. Greedy, he was near enough chocking on it.

"No, G!" Lewy cried out, but the trap triggered before he could toss the food aside. His lack of weight left lots of pull on the line, and G, shot off across the water and out of sight.

Dave Buzz reeled it in fast, forcing poor G to hurtle out of control and tear through the weeds. G, was dragged backwards, until, the line snagged around some branches with a thud. As G, came round his predicament wasn't good. Still attached to the line he was trapped, worse still, the bigger of the branches was being pulled from above. Panic set in, and G, heard a hopeful sound. Expecting to see Jenny or Lewy, he was horrified to see Jasper, the pike from the day before.

"Well, well, well, what a small pond we live in. I had a feeling our paths might cross again."

The pike, examined the branch being pulled, then G, who was pushing in the opposite direction.

“That’s red line you’re attached to,” the pike gloated, “there’s not a fish in the pond that can break that, how convenient.”

“My friends will be here any moment,” G, mumbled, “and you’ll be sorry if you hurt me.”

But his plea went unheard. Teeth revealed, Jasper the pike grinned. “Don’t worry kid this will only take a moment.”

The Pike backed up, and launched himself at G.

…

Dave Buzz, was furious at being snagged, he had the strongest line money could buy, and was prepared to pull an entire tree up if necessary. With all the strength he could muster, Dave pulled as hard as he could. Back under the water, it was as if time stood still for G. As the jaws of the big fish opened, he closed his eyes.

Then, in one synchronistic moment, the branch snapped. The pike's teeth tore through the line, which catapulted G, into the weeds, and sent Dave, sprawling back into his chair. Dazed by the event, G looked up. The Pike gone, he saw Lewy and Jenny.

"I'm over here." Hook and line hanging from his mouth, G, breathed hard.

"How on earth did you get out of that?" Lewy was astonished. "You can explain later," Jenny said, "we'd better get that hook looked at. Lewy," she asked, "would you go ahead and make an appointment with the cray specialist please?"

"Sure thing..." At an impressive speed, Lewy scuttled away. "Do you realize how lucky you are?" Jenny examined the hook, "Why won't you listen? You could have been eaten, or worse still captured by the worse god of all."

G didn't answer. Looking sorry for himself, he followed Jenny. They arrived at two vertical slates that marked the entrance to a small cave. There, Lewy was waiting for them.

"The specialist is ready," Lewy prompted, "just go in G."

Inside the cave, G was met by an eccentric cray fish with only one claw.

"Lost the other one removing a hook from a predator," the cray confirmed, "took it clean off, he did. Your, lucky kid, I don't help just anyone these days. Now, if you dare, open wide."

The cray looked carefully inside G's mouth.

"We've got a double hooked barb, this won't be easy, it may even leave a tear, but I think I can get it."

The cray wriggled the hook sideways and backwards, then with one furious twist, snapped and pulled it out. "There's only one god who uses these, and you don't want to meet him."

With a quirky smile, the cray tossed the hook onto a pile of stones, and bid G, goodbye. Outside, G was met by the others.

"Some rest I say," with that, Jenny led them to the silt beds.

…

Smithy and Dash, prepared to pack up. It had been a good day for Dash, who'd caught three big bream. But, Smithy was best pleased at having taught his son, how to tackle up and tie hooks. Walking back to the car, Smithy glanced over his shoulder at Twelve Acre. The best part of the week was still to come, and he was determined to make the most of it. Bright and early the next morning, Smithy and Dash, entered the tackle shop. There, uncle Paul, was already buying some more bait.

"Where's the picture gallery dad?"

Dash was full of excitement. Smithy pointed to the far end of the shop. There, the walls were covered in photos mainly of Dave Buzz, but his uncle Paul, was there too, holding up a huge cat fish. Uncle Paul approached Dash and pointed to the picture. “That was the night of the great storm,” he said proudly, “and to date is still the lake record for cat fish.”

“Wow…” Knowing his dad, had caught some of the biggest fish from Twelve Acre, Dash’s excitement simmered.

“But, where’s dad?”

Uncle Paul placed his hand on Dash’s shoulder. “C’mon kid, I want to show you something.”

Leaving the pictures, they leant on the counter. Above it was an antique rod. Excellent in condition, it appeared never to have been used.

“It’s a split cane masters,” uncle, Paul confirmed, “only ten were ever made. They say it was the last rod, to catch what is now known, as the legend, back in 89. The fish weighed in at 59lbs and had a small scar on its fin. Apparently, no one has ever caught it since.”

The rod and story captivated Dash. “Aider, the old chap talking to your father over there has offered a set of XP, 3000, rods, for anyone, who can again catch the legend.”

“Do you think we can do it uncle, Paul?”

“Just like your dad,” uncle, Paul laughed, “full of hopes and dreams.”

Leaving the shop, Dash questioned his father as to why there were no photos of him on the wall.

"I have awesome photos, but they are for me and my friends, otherwise fish just become trophies." Smithy paused, "Son, I don't want to be like Dave Buzz, and lose sight of why we fish in the first place."

"But did you see the picture, of uncle, Paul's cat fish? It was enormous."

"Yes..."

Smithy approached the lake. Desperate to fish the deep snag inlets, Dash tugged at his dad and pointed, "Uncle Paul is there too." Sure enough, his uncle had already set up.

Smithy felt pressured. The booming voice and loud laughter of uncle, Paul, all too often compromised his peace. But reluctant to please his son, he agreed to head for the far end.

...

Bruised and furious, that G had escaped him on more than one occasion, Jasper, the pike called a meeting. Predators in position, he recalled the events.

"A certain fish has escaped us twice, destroyed our holding facility and made us all look like fools."

"We have got to do something!" Fang, a tatty pike with a front tooth missing called out.

"But were outnumbered when it comes to the carp," Stripe a fat spiny perch added, "and they're bigger."

"It's the small carp that has to pay," another injected into the debate, "they should hand him over."

"Tyson and the elders will never hand over one of their own," the perch again added, "you know, the rules on fair game."

"Quiet," Jasper raised his voice, "if it's fair game that they want, then that's what we will give them. I feel some outside help may be required." Revealing his razor teeth something hatched in his head. "I suggest we seek out Devlan."

The very idea of asking the most monstrous fish in the pond for help made them all gasp. King of the cat fish Devlan could eat each and every one of them whole.

"But, why, would Devlan want to help us." Fang, the toothless pike, asked.

"Because, like us, he is a predator, and has a dislike for Tyson, and I, think I know a way to tempt him."

The pike ruffled the floor with their tails and roared with approval.

"Stripe and Fang," Jasper looked over to where the silt beds lay, "come with me, were going to Cat Alley."

"Why bring Stripe?" Fang wasn't pleased about the lack of muscle.

"Just because..." Jasper snapped, "now, c'mon."

A sense of dread surrounded them both, but, Stripe and Fang, followed Jasper. Passing through the jaw bone, they set off in search of the mighty, Devlan.

G was still nursing his mouth, when a sense of hunger came over him. Looking around, he spotted Jenny talking to some young carp. One of them being, the pretty young mirror, who'd previously caught his eye. As G joined them, the young fish chuckled and Jenny noticed them both blush.

"Morning," Jenny smiled at G, "how you feeling today?"

"Oh fine, well, hungry, can we find some food?"

"I think," Jenny mused moving away from the other fish, "that it's time I introduced you to the four shoals. The carp population is made of three main groups," confusion appeared on G's face. "Let me explain," said Jenny, "firstly, there is Tyson, and the Caesium shoal.

Then we got the Commons, we call them that because the bulk of the shoal, is common carp. Finally, we have my shoal known as the Natives. We're the oldest group, in the water."

"But, you and Lewy don't swim in a shoal." G, questioned her.

"Well observed. But you don't have to swim with a shoal to belong to one." Jenny was thoughtful, but it's useful in times of trouble."

"Who does Lewy belong to?" G, asked.

"The Caesium shoal…"

"Oh…" G appeared inquisitive so Jenny continued.

"There was a time, when he and Tyson weren't just close in size. Not so now though."

"But, Lewy is the best carp a fish could meet."

"The last time Lewy got caught, he spent too much time on the bank. Since then he has adopted a new attitude to life. One that Tyson doesn't like."

"And…" G, asked eagerly…

"And, Tyson pushed Lewy out of the shoal."

"So who are the biggest fish in the water?" G was beginning to find the whole thing fascinating.

"They're known as the sixty pounders, head of the Natives. Old Birdie the philosopher, he got caught many moons ago and still carries a tiny scar on his fin. Then there's Tessa, who heads the commons and of course Tyson, the biggest by far."

Taking it all in, G, was quiet.

"C'mon," Jenny snapped lightening his mood, "let's see how fast you can swim to the silt beds!"

Dash quietly made his way around to where his uncle was. "What are you fishing for uncle, Paul?" He whispered.

"Dash, I didn't hear you coming kid!" His usual loud self, Paul ignored the attempt Dash had made to observe the peace. "We're after big cats today!"

Uncle Paul unzipped his bag and held up a smelly mackerel. Disgusted by the sight, Paul was amused by the look on Dash's face.

"See that small sluice gate in the corner?" Dash followed Paul's arm. "From there, runs a silt trench, stretching nearly the length of the lake, it gets very deep, but the cats just love it."

Dash was impressed by his uncle's knowledge of the water. "So you think you might catch another monster?" Dash was referring to the record cat fish that his uncle had caught a few years ago.

"You've heard the story about Dave Buzz, and the sinking

of his boat, haven't you?" Dash nodded. "Well, people believe there's a catfish in here that weighs well over a hundred and fifty pounds. I sure would like to find out."

As he made his way back to his dad, Dash began to dream about a monster fish. Arriving at the swim he relayed his uncle's intentions, then. ..

"Do you think we can fish for cats?"

"One step at a time Dash, cat fish will eat most things including our boilies. Personally, I'm not a great fan. They are ugly looking creatures."

"Is this the spot Dave Buzz was sunk by a monster cat?"

Looking to his left, Smithy, recalled the night he´d witnessed Dave, being towed into the snags…

"It's over there, about ten feet down."

Dash looked into the dark water and a shudder went down his spine. "How deep does it get out there dad?"

Smithy paused, rubbing his chin in a contemplative manner. "Well, generally, this end of the lake is the deepest, going down about ten to twelve feet. But there are a few deeper holes close to the sluice gate."

To occupy his son's time, Smithy, set Dash the task of tying new rigs. He sat down, and not even Dave Buzz, rowing his baits straight into another man's swim, was going to spoil his peace. But on further viewing the water, Smithy couldn't help but laugh. Waist high, covered in mud, uncle, Paul, had taken one step too many into the reeds and the ground had given way and consumed him. Smithy and Dash roared with laughter. A minute later, so did his uncle.

...

Half way along Cat Alley, Fang and Stripe followed Jasper, but found no sign of Devlan.

"I have never liked this place." Stripe began to feel anxious, "it's dark, lifeless and creepy. You can see why the cat's like it."

"We cats like it down here for its peace and quiet!" A voice boomed back.

At first the fish could see nothing in the gloom, then, with an explosion of bubbles, the silt and leaves begun to move. A huge area of the trench rose up and a large pair of eyes stared at them. Dwarfing the three predators Devlan, truly was a monster.

"I hear you are looking for me?"

The three fish looked surprised. In a show of bravery, Jasper moved forward.

"We merely seek to employ your services. Help us with a delicate matter."

"Yes, Stripe piped up, "There's this carp, made us and Jasper look like a right fool he has."

Jasper threw Stripe a scolding look.

"So the carp are giving you the run around," Devlan laughed, "You surprise me." He turned to Stripe. "If it wasn't for your spiny body, I'd have eaten you for breakfast!" Stripe backed away from the dark monster. "So, what is it you want from me?"

"A disturbance during the next great frenzy," said Jasper, "once you have the bar in panic, we'll do the rest."

"And," Devlan asked, "How do you intend on rewarding my favour?"

"By shoaling the roach along this very alley..." Jasper said with a sense of confidence.

"You know the rule of the lake," Devlan smirked, "fair game only."

"You can't be serious?" Jasper expressed surprise.

"I abide by this rule," Devlan answered, "because even us cats,

are affected by the imbalance of life, but on this occasion, perhaps, I could make an exception."

"So we have a deal?" Jasper prompted.

"Perhaps, I will let you know after the next full moon, now leave me." With that, Devlan disappeared back into the silt of his lair.

When Jenny and G, arrived at the silt beds it was a really busy time of the morning. Sucking up large mouthfuls of silt, the native carp were then sieving it out through there gills.

"What's going on?" G, enquired with a whisper.

"They're, filtering our natural food sources for blood worm."

"You eat worms?" G, made Jenny laugh.

"There's more to food than what the gods give us. C'mon, I'll show you around."

"Hey, Jenny," some carp greeted her, "Do you and your friend want to join us for some morning feeding?"

"No thanks guys, you carry on."

"I've no desire to eat worms," G, sounded relieved.

"It's a very tasty risk free diet. We get a lot of washed up food from the gods too. See those guys over there?" Jenny looked to her left. Following her gaze, G, saw sorter fish, testing, then piling up the washed out food.

"Stay here. I'll go and find out if old Birdie will see us." Jenny turned around, "Please, G, stay in plain sight of the others." She then swam away.

G, moved closer to the sorters, the food didn't look fresh and had lost some of its aroma.

"You want some kid," one of them asked.

"Um, I've already had breakfast," G distanced himself, "but thanks anyway."

Moving away, he saw the silt beds, give way to rich warm weeds. A few feet on, and a single ball of food sat on the weed. G, suddenly felt hungry, and the smell…

"You, going to eat that kid…?"

G, turned to see a large carp looking at him.

"I certainly would like too." He then caught sight of Jenny. "I have to go, you have it." G swam over to her.

"There you are," Jenny tut, "listen, old Birdie has agreed to meet you. Better still," she smiled, "has agreed for you to become, a member of the shoal."

"What does that mean?"

"It means you'll have a family to look out for you! It also gives you protection under the fair game law."

G, wasn't sure about joining a shoal, but he'd come to trust Jenny and smiled in agreement.

"I'm hooked." They all suddenly heard.

It was the carp, G, had been talking too. Dragged through the sit beds, the fish flew. While the other fish scattered, G, hurried over to the weed, where the food had been. It was gone. A sense of relief swept over him. Then from behind the weeds, voices, G recognized, caught his attention. Hiding, G listened.

"You were lucky back there Stripe."

Jasper stated with a certain amount of humour in his voice. “I thought Devlan, was going to eat you.”

“Me too,” added Fang.

“So,” Stripe asked Jasper, “how do you intend on paying him?”

“Stripe,” Jasper roared, “you talk too much my spiny friend. I have no intention of giving up the roach shoals to that oversized eel, but revenge we will have.” Jasper paused, “Its quiet. The shoals must be on the move.”

G suddenly sensed the fish to be aware of his presence. Holding his breath, he gently sank deeper into the weed for cover. From there, he watched the three predators.

“What’s wrong boss?” Stripe asked.

Jasper remained still. It was the sound of the returning carp that snapped him back into the moment.

“Follow me…” Jasper then cruised away.

G wanted to know more and foolishly followed…

Passing through a huge curtain of weed, he thought he'd lost them. A little further on, and G, dropped into a clearing. There ahead, the fish appeared to be baiting one another. G, quickly moved to his left behind a large bank of weed, from there, he took cover and listened.

"Can I?" On the silt, beneath Stripe was a small dead fish, "I did see it first boss!"

"You see," Jasper turned to Fang, "our spiny friend is good for something after all. He's found us breakfast," Jasper chuckled, "give him the tail Fang."

To Jaspers amusement, Fang took the fish in his mouth, bit off the tail and tossed it over the weed bed. Only feet from it, G, froze to the spot. Moaning to himself, Stripe chased after it like a dog.

"Boss, he's here! The fish... No the carp. Yes, the carp is here!"

Face to face with Stripe, G couldn't move. Jasper and Fang turned to see what all the fuss was about.

"The carp," Stripe smiled, but his moment was short lived and the subject quickly changed.

"You're hooked!" Jasper yelled looking at the visible line hanging from Fang's mouth. The line tightened, and Fang was torn away. In a complete state of desperation, he swam straight for the surface. G seized his moment, turned and swam as fast as he could. But, smashing through the snags and weed beds, Jasper was right on his tail. G, had pushed his luck, and was now paying the price. A narrow entrance ahead, G, pushed through it and dived into the gloom of a sunken boat.

Just fitting his head inside the caves slit, Jasper, spied G.

"You can't stay in there forever!" Jasper was furious.

"One way or another, you will be my dinner."

G's heart pounded. He knew Jasper would wait. Minutes turned into hours and hours soon felt like days. Then as luck would have it, G, heard another sound.

"Excuse me," it was Jenny, "I'm, looking for a small carp."

But who was she talking too, surely not Jasper? G neared the entrance. Jasper wasn't there. Instead a large shoal of bream had arrived and were feeding.

"Jenny it's me," still no sign of Jasper, G, moved outside of the cave.

"G, where have you been? I thought I told you not to go off alone."

"It's Jasper, he was here and…"

"And luckily for you, he must have moved off when the bream came to feed." Jenny interrupted.

"He's plotting some revenge against the carp and is going to eat the roach shoals."

"Are you telling me you've been spying on the predators," Jenny was wide mouthed, "have you got a death wish, or something G?"

"I heard them plotting, they're going to hire Devlan, and..."

"You've got to learn some rules," Jenny interrupted, "and the first is, it's none of our business. Now," her tone softened, "I've arranged for old Birdie to meet with us this morning, and I

don't intend on being late."

"But..." G, stammered.

"No but, follow me please."

G put his head down and followed Jenny's lead.

...

Back on the bank, Dash watched uncle, Paul play, what he hoped, would be a large cat. He dropped everything and ran over to him.

"Do you think it's a big fish uncle Paul?"

"Well it's not a cat that's for sure!"

"How can you tell?"

"You know if it's a cat, Dash, trust me," Paul reeled it in, "but,

it looks like we've got ourselves a good sized Pike."

Sure enough, a large green looking fish floated to the surface.

"Wow," Dash gasped, "what, do you think it weighs?"

"Let's see..." Paul placed the fish on the unhooking mat, and instructed Dash where to find his scales. Lifting the fish into a sling, Paul then hooked it on the scales.

"Twenty two pounds, take one off for the sling, that's twenty one." A customary laugh followed, "less a front tooth, this fellas in good nick, let's put him back."

Smithy left his swim and joined them. "That looked like a good fish."

"Dad you should have seen it!" Smithy smiled at his son's enthusiasm.

"So how's it going in your swim?" Uncle Paul asked.

"Since Dave Buzz decided to drop in and catch that carp, slow, but that's Dave for you."

"Yes I noticed him rowing into your swim," Paul sighed, "rumour has it, that he's using barbed hooks again."

"That wouldn't surprise me," Smithy frowned, "he was caught using soap bars once to flush fish from under the snags. Why, his behaviour is tolerated is beyond me. Still, better get back, you coming Dash?"

"Dad," Dash asked, catching him up, "why would Dave Buzz, throw soap bars into the water? I thought barbed hooks were banned because they can damage the fish?"

"Barbed hooks are banned Dash. As for soap, the idea is it

will irritate their skin forcing them into the open water. It's a terrible practice, that's not only banned, but bad for the environment too."

Dash shook his head. "Dave sounds like a bad man!"

Smithy paused. "Dave was once regarded as a friend around the place, but, his obsession, to catch a sixty pounder has overcome him."

"Do you really believe such a fish exists, dad?"

"About ten years back I was baiting up not far from your uncle Paul. That's when a large carp cruised into the swim. I recognized the carp as greedy boy the lake record. I watched him just sitting there as if waiting for something. Another carp appeared and was at least ten pounds bigger. I knew if the stories were true, that it had to be the legend. So I'd say there's a good chance we got a sixty plus in the water."

"Cool..." was all Dash said.

...

Below the surface, G was annoyed that Jenny showed no interest in the plotting predators.

"It's fair game," she said over and over.

"But what is fair game?" G, asked for the umpteenth time.

"Fair game is not upsetting the balance of things."

"But how does it work?" G persisted.

"The bream and roach shoals were once depleted by the predators gorging on them. But when the big cats began guarding them for their own feeding, the predators turned, not only on each other, but us carp too. Something had to be done, so a meeting of the elders was called. The outcome was one rule that governed all of the fish, fair game. This allows the different species to swim freely and take only what is needed."

Still feeling confused, G, didn't ask anymore. Hovering ahead of them was a humungous carp, better known, as old Birdie. G, looked quizzically at the sheer size of him, but Birdie just laughed aloud.

"Do you know how I've managed to grow so old, G?"

"No sir…"

"Discipline…! The fish in this lake believe we are at the mercy of the gods. But only once, have I been pulled from this water, and that was through lack of discipline." Birdie, frowned, and all of his knowledge was woven into one crease, "and let me tell you something else, they're not gods, merely an alien species who invade our world."

"What's it like up there?" asked G.

"Above the surface you can hardly breathe and your skin tightens. Bright lights blind you, and you're wrapped and held, before being placed back in the pond. So the only god you need concern yourself with, is, discipline." G still looked confused. "If you want to survive this game, then abide by the following. No frenzies, eat natural food, and most importantly learn to outsmart the aliens. All it takes is discipline." Birdie paused for deep breaths.

"What about fair game sir?" G, pressed.

"Ah yes the house rule, everything depends on it, but it's not something that can be explained. It's something that has to be lived. " Birdie nodded to Jenny then back to G, "now, young man, feel free to feed and we'll meet again soon."

Birdie turned, and with a single swish of his tail, propelled his way through the weeds.

Slowly, drifting back into the busy predator camp, Stripe followed, Jasper.

"How did it go?" The other fish were eager for their news. "Where is Fang?" They then asked.

Jasper said nothing at first then, "Devlan will help us…" There was loud cheering.

"All we have to do," Stripe piped up, "is shoal the roach up along Cat Alley."

"Silence you fool!" but it was too late, and Jaspers audience fell silent.

"What does he mean shoal the roach up for the cats?" The predators called out.

"Devlan, requires payment for his help." Jasper responded.

"But what will we eat, "the predators continued, "and what about fair game?"

"This carp has made a fool out of us!" Jasper's face filled with rage, "It's time we sent a message out that we're not to be messed with. Yes, well shoal the roach down the alley," Jaspers voice became sarcastic, "but, if Devlan is not there to profit from it, that's a different matter altogether, isn't it?"

"You're going to double cross Devlan aren't you?" Stripe, interrupted...

"Oh I wouldn't call it that," Jasper sneered at Stripe, "during the next storm when the cats are most active, and the carp frenzy, we'll strike the gravel bar in two teams. The carp will lose, and the pond will blame the cats."

"And..." Stripe asked.

"And..." Jasper uncovered a wire cage. "I knew when this floated to the bottom that I would find a use for it."

It was actually a cray fish basket used by the fishermen. One, that Jasper, had bitten through and put away for a project such as this. The fish surrounded the cave like cage.

"Now, not only will we have revenge, but plenty of fresh food for ourselves. All we need is to rig up a weed net to pen them in with." Jaspers plan was met with optimistic cheers.

...

"So," G, persisted, "how does fair game keep the balance?"

"One season," Jenny began, "the predators shoaled the bream and roach, until there was barely any left. At first, no one cared, not until large quantities of food began to rot, and some of the fish died from eating it. Starving, the predators began attacking the larger carp, that's when fear and panic set in everywhere. A gathering was called, and elders from each species agreed that anyone found taking more than needed, would be accountable. Fair game, created a shared responsibility for the resources, ensuring a sense of peace."

"But the predators still eat us?" G responded.

"Not more than is needed, beside without fair game, the shoals would over populate the pond, and food would become scarce again. You see were all connected, what affects one will affect another."

"Have any of the elders ever been caught Jenny?"

"Not Devlan or Tyson. Devlan got hooked a few seasons ago and what a fight he put up. Not only did he pull one of the gods into the water, but brought his vessel to the bottom too."

"Do they ever bother us?" G, asked.

"They get pushy while feeding, but we've learned to leave them to it when they frenzy."

"So how am I going to survive the season?"

"Listen, and discipline."

G didn't like the sound of discipline.

...

Back on the bank, Dash had been playing a big fish for at least ten minutes.

"Steady Dash," Smithy was excited, "don't force him son. Give him the line, let him run..."

Uncle Paul's laughter announced his presence.

"It's a whopper, uncle, Paul!"

"Stay focused on what you're doing Dash," Smithy eased a net under the large carp.

"Wow, I'd say that's close on thirty pounds," uncle Paul beamed, "what an immaculate carp, a real beauty Dash! Let me grab dad's camera."

Smithy raised the net, "Let me show you how to hold it Dash!"

"Can't we hold it together dad?"

"Might be awkward, but ok let's try."

"Is this a thirty five mill camera?" Paul chuckled to himself, "you're never going to be able to post this one on Facebook!"

"Just take the picture…" Smithy insisted.

The camera clicked and the picture was stored. Leaving the fish with Dash, Smithy grabbed his scales. The fish weighed in at thirty two pounds three ounces.

"You're a natural Dash," uncle, Paul said over and over, "let's help it back into the water, shall we?"

The three of them watched the fish disappear in the darkness of the lake. Smithy yawned, then, looked at Dash.

"I think we should call it a day son."

"Yes," uncle, Paul ruffled Dash's hair, "I think I'll pack up myself."

...

As the weeks passed, G, learnt quickly from Jenny. He could soon pick and test food, map safe routes and find popular feeding spots without crossing the predators. Sunning himself, in the shallows with Jenny, G, noticed shoals of carp, roach and bream, arrive at the Gravel Bar. A frenzy begun to develop and the cray fish struggled to keep up with the piles of prepared foods. Arriving amongst them, Tyson pushed them out of his way and took what he wanted.

"Why, the frenzy?" G, asked Jenny.

"The water pressure is changing, I sense a storm."

G, paused, where had he heard that before? Then it came to him, Jasper. He watched the roach pick at crumbs and particles the big fish had stirred up. G considered telling Jenny what Jasper had said, but gave it up on the basis that she would just say, fair game. G knew what Jasper had in mind, had nothing to do with fair game, but while there were numbers, G, felt safe. Lewy appeared, and like a huge hoover sucked up large quantities of food, very nearly eating one of the cray fish too.

"Oops, sorry little fellow," Lewy frowned, but the cray fish was not amused.

"Hey, Lewy, over here," G, called out.

"Hey kid it's a frenzy, jump in!" Lewy's excitement was infectious. G was on the move when…

"Hold on there," Jenny blocked his path, "Remember the word discipline, G?"

"But the whole ponds in frenzy," G, protested.

"More fish get hooked during this crazy feeding session, than at any other time."

The word felt like a cruel joke, his natural urge was to gorge.

"Incoming, we got incoming."

Food rained down luring large shoals of roach to the surface. G had never witnessed anything like it. Slowly, he, moved towards the bar, but was knocked sideways by a large cat fish.

"G, are you ok?" It was Jenny, "once those cats start, it can get pretty rough down here."

G sensed something bad about to happen. Surely, this would be the perfect time for Jasper to strike.

As he pondered what to do, the pretty young carp he'd seen twice before approached.

"Hello," she asked.

"Hi," G responded shyly.

"Is this your first water storm frenzy?"

"Err, yes," G, was a little lost for words.

"I'm Susie, from the Cassium shoal. Do you have a name?"

"My name is Georgie, but most fish call me G. I'm with the Natives..."

"That's a shame, were not meant to mix with other shoal members."

"I've never heard of that before." G, was surprised, "I talk to other group members."

"I know I've seen you talking to Lewy, that's why he doesn't get on with Tyson."

"Well I think it's a silly rule," G, puffed his chest out, "no one tells me who I can talk to."

"You're funny," a series of giggles left Susie, "so, how come you're not feeding?"

"I need to warn the roach that Jasper and Devlan are coming." Susie giggle some more. "No, I'm serious, and no one will listen. Will you help me?"

"I get it, this is a game…"

"Yes a game, I'm looking for a large roach with a scar on his face can you find him?"

Giggling as she went, Susie swam upwards. Moving through the frantic crowd, G began to doubt if the roach was still alive. He searched everywhere he could think of, then…

"Over here, G." Susie had found the roach.

"Hey, remember me?" G approached them.

"Sure, it's my old jail break buddy," the silver fish said happily,

"I didn't think I'd see you again."

"Listen to me," G, was almost frantic, "Jasper and the cats are planning something bad, I think it's only a matter of time."

"Slow down G," the roach raised a brow, "no one's going to cause trouble tonight the whole ponds here."

"Great game," Susie interrupted, "who's next G?"

"This is no game I tell you, why you won't listen to me?"

As the words left his mouth a whole lot of catfish arrived and began tearing up the bar. Within seconds, the shoals were trying to escape the silt cloud they were caught in.

"Swim for it!" The roach shrieked taking off after the fleeing shoals.

"They're heading for a trap, Susie, this way!" But she didn't move, "come on!" G persisted.

"We can't interfere," Susie said, "we have to return to our own shoal."

"Fine, you go, but I'm going to help the roach."

Susie called after G, but he didn't stop. Susie spun around quickly to search for Lewy. Moving along the chaotic bar visibility was poor, but there he was, still gorging.

"Lewy," she called, "your friend is in some sort of trouble."

"Slow down Susie, who's in trouble?"

"It's G. He thinks the predators are planning something bad, so he took off to help the roach."

"Oh no," Lewy looked sad, "Jenny said he had this crazy notion, but..."

Lewy stopped in mid flow, behind Susie moving menacingly,

along the bar, was groups of predators. But rather than attacking, they were looking for someone.

"Susie, get back to your shoal. I will go after G."

Lewy first found Jenny. "Tell me everything, G, told you about the predators plan?"

Jenny began to explain, then, panicked in mid flow, "we need to find him!"

"Cat Alley," Said Lewy, "C'mon."

G swam fast. If he could lead them away from the alley entrance they stood a chance. The first there, an eerie silence greeted him. There was nothing, nothing but sheets of green weed and gravel. Back at the bar, Jasper, and the others searched frantically.

"Boss he isn't here, no one's seen him." Stripe insisted.

"He has to be here," jasper ordered, "look again!"

"Over here." came a voice. Jasper was faced with a scrawny looking Perch. "I've seen him, the one you're after."

"Well, do tell my friend." Jasper asked in a sarcastic tone.

"Well it was a strange sight, Pike in pursuit, the roach shoals fled, I was about to join them, when I saw a small carp follow the hunt."

"I hope your right, for your sake, or you may find yourself on my menu." Jasper rallied the pike up and headed for Cat Alley. Without any warning, the roach shoal crashed into the area, swept through the weed, and into the wire cage. Skidding after them, G found he could go no further.

“The predators,” the front roach called out, “have penned us in.”

G, looked at the wall he was flat against, sure enough, beneath the weed was a wire cage.

G pushed his way to the front where a sheet of weed now covered the entrance. Disheartened, he spotted his roach friend with the scar.

“How did this happen?” The roach asked G.

“Oh it was easy, really.” A shadow appeared on the other side of the weed sheet. A second later the weed was torn further apart and Jasper appeared. “Frenzy’s aren’t just good for feeding you know!”

Pleased with his catch, Jasper nosed the latch into place.

…

Up on the bank, it would be Dash's first night fish, and despite the looming storm, he couldn't wait to set up.

"Hey dad, there's Dave Buzz." Smithy's mood instantly dropped, squinting hard, Dash was right, tightly tucked away, in the far corner, was Dave.

"That guy," his uncle Paul, laughed, "lives here, I swear."

"Dad, are we still going to fish the snags?" Dash said in a pleading voice.

"Of course we are, come on let's get started." Determined not to let Dave Buzz bother him, Smithy unzipped his bivvy bag and passed Dash the poles. They were slotting them together, when a whoosh of laughter was heard.

"Still struggling with your old school kits I see," uncle, Paul mocked, "here, let me introduce you to the modern day pop up bivvy."

Smithy scorned, at uncle, Paul's indulgence, put his tent up and unfolded a chair.

"Here you are," Smithy, said to Dash, "you can have the new bed chair for the evening."

Comfortable, Dash watched his father lay out the rest of the equipment. He then glanced back at uncle, Paul, and saw that the pop up tent had collapsed on him. Laughing, Dash thought it was hilarious.

"It looked far easier in the advert," Paul shouted from underneath a mound of water proof plastic, "honestly it did!"

Amusement displayed, Smithy and Dash helped him put the bivvy back up. They then baited the water, cast their rods, and waited, but as night brewed, so did their thirst.

"Dash I think it's time to fire up the stove," said Smithy, "pass me the kettle please."

"Dad, is uncle, Paul, going to dine with us tonight?"

"Knowing your uncle," Smithy smirked, "he's probably got some of that astronaut food but, ask him anyway."

Dash wandered a few yards to his left. "Uncle Paul, dad wants to know if you're joining us for food."

"Self-heating food," His uncle held something up, "they use this on Everest, away with clumsy gas stoves and boiling water!"

Dash went back to his swim.

"You were right dad," he laughed, "he's got space food."

...

The sight of G, made Jasper smile, "had we known you'd be here, it would have saved us the bother of looking for you." G, appeared puzzled. "He still doesn't get it," Jasper's teeth glistened, "all this was just for you, my little nuisance. It's called revenge!"

G's mind raced, it seemed that his actions had driven the predators to break fair game.

"But what about the roach…?" G shouted through the bars and torn weed at Jasper.

"Let's call them an added bonus." The predators laughed but a more sinister one boomed above theirs.

"You weren't thinking about double crossing me, were you Jasper?"

"Devlan," Jasper stammered in fear, "the roach, as promised."

Three more big cats arrived onto the scene. Watching the events unfolding, G came up with a loose idea he whispered to the roach. Slowly the idea filtered back to all the fish. "We'll have the carp," Jasper mused, "and you the roach. Maybe, it's time to tuck in."

"Oh Jasper you have been a naughty boy," Devlan was unimpressed, "Whatever happened to fair game."

"But I thought…" Jasper was feeling uneasy.

"You thought what I wanted you to think," Devlan's smile darkened. "My part in this game serve's a different purpose. Other fish will be here soon and the games will commence."

"Everyone…?" Jasper enquired in a rather uneasy tone.

"Yes Jasper. Look..." A large carp followed by a dozen others approached, "how punctual."

"Tyson…!" G, gasped.

"What is the meaning of this Devlan?" Tyson was in no mood to be trifled with. "You know the law of the water!"

"Ah good of you to join us," Devlan was enjoying himself, "we appear to have a situation, created by our friends from let's say the shadier parts of the water."

"There is no situation, you know the rules," Tyson was mad, "so I suggest you open that cage," he glared at Jasper, "and let the fish disperse immediately."

"Tyson," Devlan chuckled to himself, "Tyson the great un-hooked fish, still giving out his orders. This situation has little bearing on us cats. For us this is fair game, unless…"

"Unless what," Tyson snapped.

"We play a different game, one that involves me and you."

"Out of the question," Tyson snapped.

"Then I guess," Devlan grinned, "it's time we served up dinner, starting with the little carp."

There, on the other side of the weed, bunched in with the roach, Tyson spied G.

"Wait," the tone of Tyson was calmer, "what is your game?"

"Frenzy roulette..!" Devlan had never looked more devious. "At the edge of the alley, the gods have deposited a large quantity of food. I would guess somewhere in it, is a trap. Our job is to spring the trap through gorging. If I get hooked you all go free, but if you get hooked, well let's just say every fish becomes fair game. "

As every fish present looked to Tyson, the tension in the water grew.

"Let's do it." Tyson gave Devlan a menacing stare and turned towards the alley.

Jasper knew that neither had been taken from the water and that Devlan, was desperate to see Tyson hooked. Resentful that he'd had used him to get at Tyson, Jasper was furious. Flicking his tail he moved nearer to the alley. Amongst the fish arriving to watch, was Lewy and Jenny.

"The kids trapped," Lewy whispered.

"Don't worry," Jenny said quietly, "when the frenzy begins, I will go and undo the cage. At least then if Tyson loses, they can make a run for it."

Either side of the food, giving each other horrible looks, the two big fish circled it over and over.

"There is only one rule," Devlan shouted for all the shoals to hear, "let the frenzy begin."

Like two vacuum cleaners, the big fish began funnelling food as if it were their last.

…

As the first drops of rain began to fall, uncle, Paul scooped up his chair and brolly, and hurried over to the others in time for supper. While Smithy stirred soup, Paul ate space food and shared his stories with Dash.

"Do you think carp are intelligent uncle, Paul?"

"Well it does make you wonder, when they eat every morsel from the surface but don't touch the bait."

"What I want to know," Smithy, said, "is how the fish always know you're about to eat or do something when you get a run."

"They sure do pick their moments," Paul laughed aloud making Smithy wince at the noise.

"Hey," Dash shouted, "the water is fizzing with bubbles where we baited earlier."

Smithy stood up followed by uncle, Paul.

"The Boys right," Paul mused, "there must be a whole shoal of fish out there feeding, looks like we best throw some more out." Smithy winced once more. He'd not been overly happy about the bucket loads already tipped in by Paul.

"Let's just settle," Smithy suggested, "finish our food then see what's what."

"Could be a missed opportunity, if this rain kicks in..."

Before Smithy could comment, Dash's bight alarm went screaming off.

"You're in son, strike it!"

...

The fact Tyson had not backed down came as a big surprise to Jenny and Lewy. He'd always been an uncaring arrogant lord of the gravel bar, yet, here he was, putting himself on the line for the roach, and a small carp from a different shoal. Jenny moved backwards until she was touching the cage.

"G, tell me if Jasper turns around."

"Ok, I'm on it."

Nuzzling the latch, Jenny pushed it upwards until it popped over the edge.

"Tell the fish to be ready to run G."

"I've already told the fish to follow me."

Jenny then swam back to Lewy.

There was tension amongst the fish especially the roach whose fate depended on the outcome. Devlan and Tyson were gorging furiously when without warning a huge cry sounded out.

"Tyson is hooked!" Lewy yelled.

G, caught the eye of Jasper, a moment later all hell broke loose and carp crashed the scene, cats kicked up clouds of silt and Predators, took off like missiles in the direction, G, had fled. Leading the roach as fast as he could through the alley, G saw the cave he was searching for. Not far behind, Jasper was snapping at the tails of the roach.

"Quickly inside..." G was anxious, "come on," he squealed, "you've got to make it!" But the Pike were quick and only seconds away from taking out the shoal. Knowing it was him the pike wanted, G, took off. Without hesitation, Jasper and his cronies took after him. G skimmed the rocks and dodged past numerous snags, exhausted, he headed for curtain of weed.

Unable to weave through the hanging green maize, he became stuck. From behind him, pursuing pike crashed into the weed. G tried to turn, but his fins were too tangled.

"He's mine," Jasper called out, "this is one situation you won't come back from my annoying little friend." His voice was full of anger.

"Jasper..." Stripes squeaky voice came from behind him.

"What is it Stripe," Jasper seethed, "you are always interrupting me."

"Boss, I don't think we want to be here."

Jasper noticed the other predators backing away. A swish of his tail, and he turned around to be confronted by, Birdie, Susie, and the entire Caesium shoal.

"Now, Jasper, you listen, and listen well. If I even hear you've been within a weed bed of this young carp," Birdie looked upon G, "I will personally, make sure, you, and the rest of your clan, wish you'd never been born! Do you understand?"

Jasper boiled with rage, "it's not fair," he scorned, but knew to go against the carp shoals would be futile. Slowly, very slowly he turned, looking back once with a defeated glare before disappearing into the gloom.

...

Dash had struck hard. His rod bent and almost doubled. Pulling him from his feet, his uncle had to steady him. The line continued to rip from his reel.

"Tighten that clutch Dash," Smithy yelled, "he's taking the line too easily."

But the sheer strength of the fish pulled him off balance again. "I can't dad, he's too strong."

"Steady yourself and let him take the line then." Smithy insisted.

"Listen to your dad kid," uncle, Paul added, "I reckon that's a big fish." The line continued to rip from his reel.

"He's heading for the far side dad, I just can't slow him."

"Don't panic Dash, if he needs line that's cool, just try and turn him slightly like I've shown you."

Dash struggled to turn the fish in the rain. He could hear a bite alarm. Somehow, the fish had taken him through one of Dave Buzz's rods.

"Ignore the alarm," Smithy shouted, "just keep trying to do the right thing. Paul, bring those other rods in for me."

"Sure…"Paul brought the rods in and made room for Dash, but along with the faint rumble of thunder, the rain continued.

Believing it to be a fish, Dave tore out of his tent, quickly seeing it wasn't, he rained curses on those opposite him.

"Just ignore him son. Paul, you'd better get around there and see what you can do to help."

"Don't worry Dash," carrying a look of concern, Paul began the walk towards Dave, "I'll be back before you know it."

Dash continued trying to turn the large fish until the line stopped streaming from his reel.

"I think he's trying to swim back towards us dad."

"That's ok, keep the line and reel tight as he does."

Dash kept the tension just as he'd been taught, but his arm was beginning to ache.

"Just hold him, don't force him, by the look of the bend in your rod it could be a cat fish."

"Feels like one dad."

Dash saw a bad tempered argument break out between his uncle and Dave Buzz, both of them now throwing their arms into the air. Then a very peculiar thing happened.

"Dad, I think I've lost him, the lines gone slack."

"Keep reeling son," Smithy encouraged.

"Wait up, I've got something, but his fish stopped fighting." The bend in his rod lessoned, and it took a few minutes to take back the line, that had been pulled from his reel. Just then his uncle returned.

"Is Dave alright?" Dash asked.

"Don't worry about him," uncle, Paul said, "Dave won't be bothering us again tonight."

Dash looked across at Dave, and for a moment felt sorry for him. His obsession for the lake record had helped shape the man.

"Dash, we still got a fish to land, remember?" Smithies words brought Dash back into focus and he continued to reel.

Two rod lengths out, and a swirl told him the fish was close.

"Dash it's a carp," Smithy yelled, "a big one at that. Pass me the landing net Paul."

As Dash struggled to bring the fish closer, uncle, Paul handed Smithy the landing net.

"Easy Dash," uncle Paul encouraged, "you're doing great, let your dad move the net under him."

Smithy entered the water to extend his reach, "come on Dash, just a little more, you've got a…" Smithy pulled the net inwards, "Oh my god, Dash, it's a monster, here, Paul take this."

He passed the net up to Paul who struggled to lift the large fish from the water. Paul placed the carp on the unhooking mat, and

"Dash I think it's the legend," Smithy was dumbstruck, "Paul, where are those amazing scales you're always telling me about?"

"I'll go and get them…"

Dash knelt and gently removed the hook from its mouth. He looked across the lake, but could see no sign of Dave. Again, Dash felt sorry for him. Paul returned with the scales and lifted the fish onto them.

"Seventy two pounds…!" Smithy mumbled, in a disbelieving voice.

"I've got to get the camera for this one." Paul turned around, "Dash you've caught the legend, you're going to have your photo up in the shop!"

"Wait," Dash looked at his father, then across the lake once more, "I want to put him back without the photo."

"But it's the lake record," his uncle Paul interrupted.

“Fish, are not trophies uncle, Paul. If, everyone knows they will all come here and try to catch him!”

“But, a moment like this may never come along again,” Paul looked to Smithy for support, “tell him, will you.”

“Son, if that’s what you feel,” Smithy smiled, “then let’s put him back.”

“Is that what I think it is?” All three of them turned in disbelief to see Dave Buzz.

“Yes, and I`m about to let him go, would you like to help me?” Dash asked much to the astonishment of his uncle and farther.

“Could I?” Dave looked taken back, almost embarrassed by the heartfelt boy before him.

Smithy was humbled by his son’s openness and smiled at Dave, “Sure, go ahead.”

Smithy and Paul watched them lower the giant fish back into the water. For Smithy, to see Dave have a change of heart and become a fellow fisherman again was not only the highlight of that summer, but his whole fishing career.

…

It was the morning after the great rain storm that G, woke and began badgering Jenny.

"What happened," he asked her, "did the roach escape, and where's Tyson?"

"Slow down G, one thing at a time," Jenny replied.

"But, Tyson was hooked."

"Lewy," Jenny nudged her companion, "perhaps you could explain better."

"After you took off with the roach," Lewy began, "a lot of us big carp followed Tyson. And let me tell you, I've never seen a hooked fish swim like him. He must have nearly pulled the god into the water. Everyone knows if you're going to break a hold, you have to pace yourself. But, the poor fellow went from one side of the lake to the other, sadly, exhausted by his sheer size, he just gave up."

"But, why did he help?" G, enquired, "I thought Tyson only cared about himself?"

"Well, G, you got a certain young carp to thank for that. Susie, just so happens to be his niece. She reminded Tyson that he has a responsibility, not just to his own shoal, but to all of the carp."

"Where is every one now?" G, asked.

"Thought you might ask that," Jenny interrupted, "come on, follow us."

Taking a familiar route, they came out into the clearing. There, crowding the bar were shoals of carp, tench, bream, roach and rudd.

Amongst them, he saw Birdie and Tyson. “What’s going on?” G, whispered.

“They’re all here to honour you kid,” Lewy whispered, “Your actions have united the shoals, even Tyson.”

“Go ahead,” Jenny nudged G, forward, “this is your moment.”

Slowly, and shyly, G swam towards the bar. Surrounded, he was quickly swamped in cheering. A pretty carp approached. “Someone is popular.”

“Susie,” G, cried out with delight.

“Well,” she smiled, “looks like you’re on a winner today.”

www.bonkerbooks.com
bonkerbookswriting@gmail.com

www.ingramcontent.com/pod-product-compliance
Lightning Source LLC
LaVergne TN
LVHW060615110826
845154LV00003B/93
* 9 7 8 0 9 9 2 9 1 4 4 5 5 *